E FICTION PAL

Palmisciano, Diane.

Garden partners

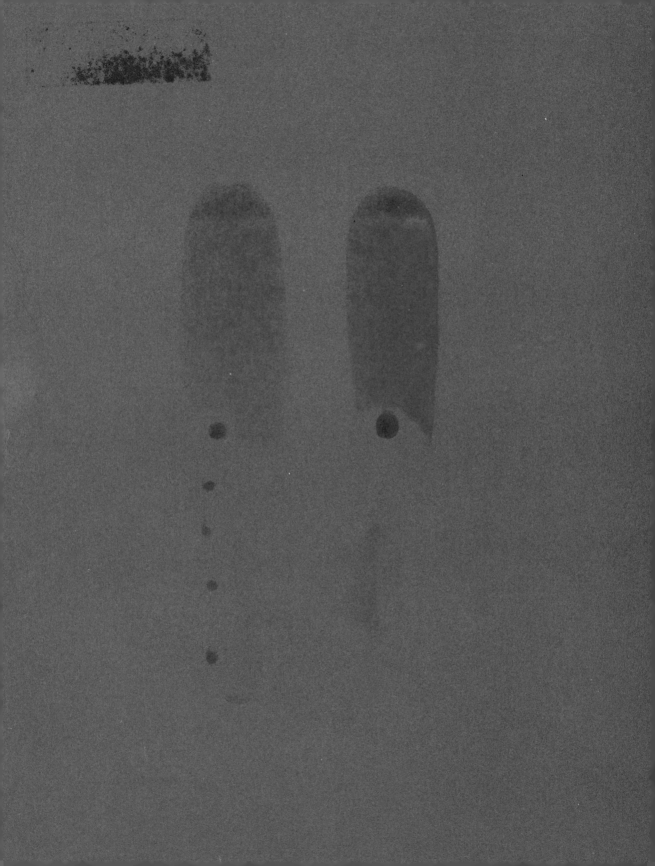

Garden Partners

Diane Palmisciano

ATHENEUM   1989   NEW YORK

E
FICTION
PAL

Atheneum
Macmillan Publishing Company
866 Third Avenue, New York, NY 10022
Collier Macmillan Canada, Inc.
First Edition
Printed in Hong Kong by South China Printing Co.
10 9 8 7 6 5 4 3 2 1

Library of Congress Cataloging-in-Publication Data
Palmisciano, Diane.
Garden partners.
Summary: A child and her grandmother plant seeds,
care for their garden all summer, and share the
harvest with friends and family.
[1. Grandmothers—Fiction. 2. Gardens—Fiction] I. Title.
PZ7.P1874Gar 1989 [E] 88-16741
ISBN 0-689-31415-9

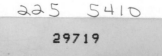

To the memory
of my grandmother Cristina

When the front door thumps shut and the car whirs down the driveway, I know I have Gram all to myself. Tap, tap, tap, I signal to Gram on my bedroom wall. Tap, tap, she answers. It's time to get up.

We wash and dress and then we are ready for breakfast. Gram shows me how to unwind an orange peel in one long curly strip.

"This would make a good tail for an orange pig," she says. Gram sips her coffee very slowly.

"Can we go now?" I ask.

"First things first," says Gram. She takes the dishes to the sink. I wipe the jelly off the table.

"Are you ready?" she asks.

I run for the door. We are going to start our garden!

Right now it doesn't look like a garden. It looks like a blank piece of dirt. "With a little planning and a lot of work," Gram says, "it will be the best garden ever."

"Daddy likes lots of tomatoes and Mommy always wants flowers," I say. "My favorite is the curly kind of lettuce."

"We can put flowers along the edge," says Gram, "tomatoes in the center, corn and potatoes in the north corner, and cucumbers and curly lettuce on the south side."

Gram and I go to Mr. Jackson's store to buy our seeds. Gram takes a long time studying each package. Our neighbor, Mrs. Santoro, comes in and tells us she has ordered her seeds from a catalog this year.

"They guarantee good results," she says. "You're wasting your time buying these seeds."

Gram smiles and keeps on studying the packages. When Mrs. Santoro leaves, Gram tells me, "Seeds are seeds. It's part soil, part weather, and most of all hard work that makes a good garden."

Before we can plant anything, we have to dig and hoe to turn over the soil. Mrs. Santoro comes by and watches for a while.

"It will go much faster if you rent some equipment," she says.

"Preparation takes time," Gram says. "This first step can't be rushed."

"Why couldn't we plant the seeds today?" I ask later.

"We have to wait until the moon's not full," says Gram. "Always plant after the full moon. If you don't wait, you'll get tall plants but no fruit."

Gram tells me stories about gardening when she was little, with her donkey named Violet.

Soon we're both so tired that we fall asleep on the couch.

The next day, Gram marks each row with a string tied to two stakes. She follows the string with her hoe so each row is neat and straight. Then we both drop in the seeds and cover them with dirt.

"This keeps them warm," Gram says, "just like a blanket."

Gram puts me in charge of watering the garden.

"Gently," Gram says. "Too much water too fast makes the seeds jump. They shouldn't jump. They should sit back and enjoy their drink."

To help us remember where each vegetable is, we mark the rows with the packages the seeds came in. We plant marigolds along each edge of the garden to keep out rabbits. Rabbits hate the smell of marigolds.

Every day we watch and wait for our first sprout.
"When will we see one, Gram?" I ask.
"Only the seeds know when they're ready," Gram says.
"Waiting is a big part of gardening."
"A really big part," I say.

It seems like years, but finally our first sprout pops up.
Then, in what seems like seconds, there are sprouts
everywhere.

Every day we weed and water and watch our garden growing greener and taller. Sometimes Gram talks to the plants because she says it helps them grow.

One day a snake slithers into our garden. Gram says snakes are good for a garden because they eat insects. But we're working, so she smacks the ground with her hoe and scares him away.

Now the plants are so tall that Gram and I can hardly see each other. The tomatoes, cucumbers, carrots, peppers, and curly kind of lettuce are finally ready. It's time for our first harvest.

"Well, partner," Gram says, "let's celebrate with a harvest supper."

"We can surprise Mommy and Daddy," I say.

Gram invites all our neighbors. Mrs. Santoro will be here too. I bring in the last of the vegetables. The neighborhood dogs stare through the kitchen screen door and wag their tails. Mommy and Daddy will be home from work soon.

When our guests arrive they bring something from their gardens too. Baskets of tomatoes, bowls of salad, and jars of peppers crowd the table. Mommy and Daddy can't stop smiling. Everyone talks about gardening and swaps stories.

"We've had small cucumbers this year," says Mrs. Santoro.

"That's too bad," says Gram. "We've had good luck with ours." Gram gives me a wink and a smile.

That night I help Gram take down her hair.
"What a wonderful harvest supper," says Gram.
"It sure was," I say. "I can't wait for the corn and
potatoes to be ready. Then we can celebrate again."